Contents

COLOUR FIRST READER books are perfect for beginner readers. All the text inside this Colour First Reader book has been checked and approved by a reading specialist, so it is the ideal size, length and level for children learning to read.

Series Reading Consultant: Prue Goodwin
Honorary Fellow of the University of Reading

Chapter One

As the children arrived at the
village school, they gazed
proudly at the long, colourful
banner hanging above the main
door.

"It looks brilliant!" cried
Hannah.

"It should do," said Tom. "We
spent ages painting it."

Rebecca sighed. "I'll be very sad if our little school really has to close."

"No more school . . ." Tom said dreamily. "I could stay in bed all day!"

"They won't let you do that," Rebecca said, pulling a face. "We'd have to go to that big horrible school in town instead."

"By bus!" Hannah said in disgust. "Yuk!"

Michael came into the
playground to ring the bell.
CLANG! CLANG! DING!
DONG!

"OK, OK, Michael, we've heard it," Tom grinned. "I reckon you've woken up the whole of Great Catesby by now."

11

The small group of seven- and eight-year-olds sat on the carpet around their teacher.

"We're going to have a new boy in our class today," Mrs Roberts told them. "He wasn't very happy at his old school, so let's make sure that he will like it here with us."

Michael put his hand up. "He won't be here for long if the place is gonna close soon!" he said cheekily.

The teacher frowned at him. "We'll all be doing our best to stop that from happening."

"But how can we stop it?" Hannah blurted out.

"It won't be easy," Mrs Roberts admitted. "But we mustn't give up hope of finding a way to save our lovely school."

Rebecca couldn't help bursting into song. It was the latest hit single by her favourite pop star, the Red Fox.

"Never give up, never give up,
Stop your crying, you gotta keep
on trying,
Something will turn up — will
always turn up . . ."

The others joined in the
chorus.
"Something will turn up — will
always turn up . . ."

Something did at that very moment. With the children in full voice, the classroom door was pushed open and Miss Jackson, the headteacher, walked in.

The song faded away, as one by one, they stared at the little boy with ginger hair standing next to her. He had a football tucked under his arm.

"I wish you would all sing as well as that in assembly," Miss Jackson said with  a smile and then introduced their new classmate. "This is Jonty. Say hello, everyone."

The boy gave them a wide, toothy grin and the ice was broken.

"Hello, Jonty!" they all chorused.

"Hi!" he beamed, and suddenly bounced the ball on the floor. "Anybody here like to play football?"

They all laughed. "Welcome, Jonty," Mrs Roberts greeted him warmly. "It seems like you've come to the right place. This lot of mine are totally soccer-mad."

Chapter Two

Jonty's arrival at Great Catesby was well timed. Mrs Roberts was planning to enter a class team in a five-a-side football tournament especially for their age-group.

"You live in that big house
outside the village, don't you?"
Michael said to him one day.
"Are your parents rich?"

Jonty gave a shrug. "Haven't
got a mum. And Dad's away a
lot. I don't see much of him."

"Who looks after you then?" asked Rebecca, trying to work out what it was about Jonty that seemed so familiar to her.

"Gran does," he said. "And we've got a housekeeper too."

"I'd rather be a goalkeeper!" grinned Hannah.

★

The first practice for the Fives
was held later that week. Most
of the class took part, hoping to
be picked for the team.

"It will be mixed, won't it?" asked Hannah. "Girls too."

"Of course," said Mrs Roberts. "You're our best goalie."

"Out of all the girls, maybe," Imran whispered to Tom. "But not the best in the whole class. That's me."

"You'll have to prove it, Imran," Tom smirked. "She's good."

Jonty took his own leather
ball to the practice and he was
the first one to score with it as
well. His shot was low and hard
and the ball fizzed just out of
reach of Hannah's dive.

 Hannah was more upset by Imran's laughter at the other end than she was at letting the goal in. And she soon made up for it. She saved another effort from Jonty and then stopped a close-range header from Tom on the line.

Hannah threw the ball out to Rebecca on the wing to start their own team's next attack.

Rebecca had won the sprint
race on Sports Day and was
too quick for anyone to catch
her, even running with the ball
at her feet.

She curled the ball over into the goalmouth, but it floated right into Imran's arms. Or at least it should have done. Imran took his eye off the ball at the last moment and let it slip between his legs into the goal. He was so embarrassed, he held his head in his hands.

"Careful, Imran!" yelled Tom.
"You might drop that too!"

Imran decided he didn't want
to play in goal after all. He
was better out on the pitch as
a defender.

When the practice finished,
Rebecca had a sudden
brainwave. "Why don't we ask
people to sponsor us in the
Fives?" she suggested. "We could
raise a lot of money for the
school."

"Great idea!" said Tom. "But what about kit? We can't all wear different colours."

"That is a problem," agreed Mrs Roberts. "I'm afraid the school can't afford to buy a team strip."

"I'll see if my dad might be able to help," Jonty piped up, making himself even more popular. "He's a big football fan."

Rebecca nodded. "I bet that's not all he is either," she said under her breath.

A wild rumour had begun to snake around the village that a famous pop star had recently moved into the area. Nobody thought that it could possibly be true — apart from Rebecca . . .

Chapter Three

The children could not believe their eyes. A man with bright red hair had just walked into their classroom.

But it wasn't his hair colour
that gave them such a shock.
It was because they recognized
him. He was the Red Fox!

Only Mrs Roberts and Jonty
were expecting his visit.

The Red Fox was holding a large cardboard box. "Got some stuff here for all you star footballers," he said with a grin.

The pop star tipped the box upside down and lots of soccer kit tumbled out on to the floor.

He grabbed one of the red shirts and held it up for everyone to see.

It had a big white capital G on the front and the name GREATS printed across the back above the number.

"G is for Great – and that's
what you'll be in the Fives!"
he cried before breaking into
a chant. *"C'mon, you Greats!
C'mon, you Greats!"*

The children were still too stunned to know what to do until Rebecca joined in and then the rest followed. Their loud chanting echoed around the school – and probably halfway around Great Catesby as well.

"C'mon, you Greats! C'mon, you Greats!"

When the Red Fox had gone, Jonty was surrounded.

"Is he really your dad?" Tom demanded. "You could have told us!"

Jonty smiled shyly. "I wanted

to keep it a secret for a while. I hoped you wouldn't all be friends with me just because of who my dad is."

"With your name being Fox and your ginger hair, we should have guessed," said Hannah.

"I already did," Rebecca claimed. "And last night I found I've even got a picture of Jonty in my Red Fox scrapbook. I knew I'd seen him somewhere before."

"Becky's fallen in love with Jonty!" Imran teased her. Rebecca ignored him.

"Incredible!" she sighed. "I've just been singing along with the Red Fox!"

"He's only Jonty's dad," Imran sneered.

"*Only!*" she sneered back. "He's the best pop singer in the world."

"Well, my dad sings pretty well too – in the bath."

"Yeah, but I don't have a poster of your dad on my bedroom wall," she laughed. "Especially not one of him in the bath!"

After another soccer practice, Mrs Roberts chose a squad of six players for the tournament so that they had a substitute for each game. She wrote the names on the entry form.

FIVE-A-SIDE COMPETITION
- Entry Form -
Tom (captain) Hannah Rebecca
Jonty Michael Imran

The whole school had a special reason for hoping that the team did well. The Red Fox was so pleased by how quickly Jonty had settled in that he was sponsoring the Greats too.

Not for just a few pence per goal. Not even for a pound a goal like some generous people in the village. For as much as a thousand pounds for every goal that they scored!

Jonty's only disappointment
was that his dad wouldn't be able
to watch them play in the Fives.
He was setting off on a concert
tour with his band.

"I'll be thinking of you, Jonty-boy," his dad promised before he left. "Show 'em who's the soccer star of the Fox family."

Jonty managed a weak smile.

"I really like it at this school, Dad. If it's closed, I might have to go back to that horrible boarding school where I was bullied."

"There'll be no going back there, don't worry. I'll see to that, OK?"

"C'mon, you Greats!" they sang happily together.

Chapter Four

"Fantastic! We're in the quarter-
finals now," cried Tom.

The captain's second goal
had just clinched his team's 2-0
victory, their third win in a row.

The Greats were enjoying
themselves so much, they'd
almost forgotten about all the
money they were earning for
the school.

"Wish my dad could have
been here to see us," said Jonty.

There was a sudden stir of
excitement in the crowd as
a helicopter began to circle
overhead. It looked as if it was
going to land on the playing
fields.

It did. Everyone felt the gusts
of wind from the whirling
blades, and then a red-haired
figure in a brown suit stepped
down from the helicopter and
ran towards them.

The Red Fox was soon
surrounded by autograph-
hunters.

"Hope I'm not too late," he
called out to the Greats.

Inspired by his flying visit,
they hit top form and the red
shirts swarmed all over their
opponents in the next match.

Goals from Rebecca, Michael and Jonty swept them easily into the semi-finals.

"C'mon, you Greats!" cheered their fans, led by the Red Fox himself. He jumped nearly as high as his helicopter when Jonty scored the third goal!

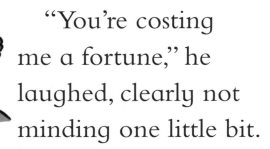

"You're costing me a fortune," he laughed, clearly not minding one little bit.

The semi-final game was much tougher. The score was locked at 0-0 until the last minute, and that's when Hannah pulled off a magnificent save to rescue her team.

A goal looked certain.

A shot was deflected off Imran's knee, but Hannah twisted round and hurled herself through the air to fingertip the ball over the crossbar.

"What a save!" cried Imran. "Thanks, Hannah. I take back all I've said. You're magic in goal!"

Tom headed the corner out of danger towards Rebecca and the Greats launched a swift breakaway raid. As Rebecca raced up the pitch, Jonty matched her for pace and he burst past his marker to reach her pass first. He smacked the ball from just outside the keeper's area and it screamed into the goal.

Jonty disappeared under a pile of teammates as they mobbed him. Only Hannah stayed out of the crush of bodies.

"We're in the final!" she yelled. "We've made it!"

There wasn't much time for the players to rest before the final, but they were too excited to feel tired yet. They were up against the tournament favourites, the Fab Five, a strong team from the biggest school in the county.

The Greats didn't care who they were playing. They rocked the Fab Five straight from the kick-off when Imran's long-range shot whistled only a fraction wide of the target. And

with a little luck, they might
have been leading by more than
1-0 at half-time. Rebecca scored
their goal, sliding home the
rebound after Tom's volley had
struck a post.

The second half, sadly, told
a different story. Once the Fab
Five had equalized, the Greats
struggled to survive a storm of
fierce attacks. Just when it

looked like they might hang on for a draw, their defence was finally cracked.

Not even Hannah could keep out the winning goal. She'd already blocked one shot and was helpless on the ground as the ball was lashed back past her into the net.

"Never mind," said Mrs Roberts after the squad received their silver medals as runners-up. "You all played your best and nobody can ask for more than that."

"But we didn't win," sighed Rebecca, almost in tears, despite the fact that they'd scored a total of ten goals.

"Cheer up!" said the Red Fox. "There's always another day."

"Not for our school, there won't be," grunted Tom.

The pop star began to sing.

"Never give up, never give up, Something will turn up, will always turn up . . ."

"I know what can turn up, Dad," cried Jonty. "A song! Why don't you make a record with all the kids at Great Catesby? That could raise loads more money to help save the school."

Everyone thought that was a wonderful idea – including the Red Fox. He ruffled his son's ginger hair.

"Right, let's do it, Jonty-boy,"
he grinned. "If it did the trick,
it'd be an even greater save than
Hannah's!"

Jonty started up their chant
again and the footballers really
had something to sing about
now. Mrs Roberts laughed in
delight. "It sounds
like we've got the
title for our song
already!"

*"C'mon, you
Greats! C'mon
you Greats!"*

THE END

Colour First Readers

Welcome to Colour First Readers. The following pages are intended for any adults (parents, relatives, teachers) who may buy these books to share the stories with youngsters. The pages explain a little about the different stages of learning to read and offer some suggestions about how best to support children at a very important point in their reading development.

Children start to learn about reading as soon as someone reads a book aloud to them when they are babies. Book-loving babies grow into toddlers who enjoy sitting on a lap listening to a story, looking at pictures or joining in with familiar words. Young children who have listened to stories start school with an expectation of enjoyment from books and this positive outlook helps as they are taught to read in the more formal context of school.

Cracking the code

Before they can enjoy reading for and to themselves, all children have to learn how to crack the alphabetic code and make meaning out of the lines and squiggles we call letters and punctuation. Some lucky pupils find the process of learning to read undemanding; some find it very hard.

Most children, within two or three years, become confident at working out what is written on the page. During this time they will probably read collections of books which are graded; that is, the books introduce a few new words and increase in length, thus helping youngsters gradually to build up their growing ability to work out the words and understand basic meanings.

Eventually, children will reach a crucial point when, without any extra help, they can decode words in an entire book, albeit a short one. They then enter the next phase of becoming a reader.

Making meaning

It is essential, at this point, that children stop seeing progress as gradually 'climbing a ladder' of books of ever-increasing difficulty. There is a transition stage between building word recognition skills and enjoying reading a story. Up until now, success has depended on getting the words right but to get pleasure from reading to themselves, children need to fully comprehend the content of what they read. Comprehension will only be reached if focus is put on understanding meaning and that can only happen if the reader is not hesitant when decoding. At this fragile, transition stage, decoding should be so easy that it slowly becomes automatic. Reading a book with ease enables children to get lost in the story, to enjoy the unfolding narrative at the same time as perfecting their newly learned word recognition skills.

At this stage in their reading development, children need to:

- Practice their newly established early decoding skills at a level which eventually enables them to do it automatically

- Concentrate on making sensible meanings from the words they decode

- Develop their ability to understand when meanings are 'between the lines' and other use of literary language

- Be introduced, very gradually, to longer books in order to build up stamina as readers

In other words, new readers need books that are well within their reading ability and that offer easy encounters with humour, inference, plot-twists etc. In the past, there have been very few children's books that provided children with these vital experiences at an early stage. Indeed, some children had to leap from highly controlled teaching materials to junior novels.

This experience often led to reluctance in youngsters who were not yet confident enough to tackle longer books.

Matching the books to reading development

Colour First Readers fill the gap between early reading and children's literature and, in doing so, support inexperienced readers at a vital time in their reading development. Reading aloud to children continues to be very important even after children have learned to read and, as they are well written by popular children's authors, Colour First Readers are great to read aloud. The stories provide plenty of opportunities for adults to demonstrate different voices or expression and, in a short time, give lots to talk about and enjoy together.

Each book in the series combines a number of highly beneficial features, including:

- Well-written and enjoyable stories by popular children's authors

- Unthreatening amounts of print on a page

- Unrestricted but accessible vocabularies

- A wide interest age to suit the different ages at which children might reach the transition stage of reading development

- Different sorts of stories – traditional, set in the past, present or future, real life and fantasy, comic and serious, adventures, mysteries etc.

- A range of engaging illustrations by different illustrators

- Stories which are as good to read aloud to children as they are to be read alone

All in all, Colour First Readers are to be welcomed for children throughout the early primary school years – not only for learning to read but also as a series of good stories to be shared by everyone. I like to think that the word 'Readers' in the title of this series refers to the many young children who will enjoy these books on their journey to becoming lifelong bookworms.

Prue Goodwin

Honorary Fellow of the University of Reading

Helping children to enjoy *Great Save*

If a child can read a page or two fluently, without struggling with the words at all, then he/she should be able to read this book alone. However, children are all different and need different levels of support to help them become confident enough to read a book to themselves.

Some young readers will not need any help to get going; they can just get on with enjoying the story. Others may lack confidence and need help getting into the story. For these children, it may help if you talk about what might happen in the book.

Explore the title, cover and first few illustrations with them, making comments and suggestions about any clues to what might happen in the story. Read the first chapter aloud together. Don't make it a chore. If they are still reluctant to do it alone, read the whole book with them, making it an enjoyable experience.

The following suggestions will not be necessary every time a book is read but, every so often, when a story has been particularly enjoyed, children love responding to it through creative activities.

Before reading

Great Save is a story based on an ordinary class in a

small country primary school. Discuss the similarities and the differences between your child's school and the one in the story. You could also talk about what it feels like to be a new child in an established class.

During reading

Asking questions about a story can be really helpful to support understanding but don't ask too many – and don't make it feel like test on what has happened. Relate the questions to the child's own experiences and imagination. For example, ask: 'Do you play football at school?', 'What must it be like having a pop star for your dad?' or 'Do you think the Greats will win the five-a-side football tournament?' With enthusiastic footballers you can have conversations about their best games. What advice would they give this school team?

Responding to the book

If your child has enjoyed this story, it increases the fun by doing something creative in response. If possible, provide art materials and dressing up clothes so that they can make things, play at being characters, write and draw, act out a scene or respond in some other way to the story.

Activities for children

If you have enjoyed reading this story, you could:

- Find the words in Chapter 1 to fill the spaces in these sentences:

   1. The school is in the village of Great _____.

   2. Mrs _____ is the name of the teacher.

   3. The new boy, called Jonty, has _____ hair and a _____ under his arm.

   4. Miss Jackson is the name of the _____.

   5. Rebecca's favourite singer is called the _____ _____.

- Ask some friends to play five-a-side football with you. Do you know the rules? You can look them up on the Internet. Perhaps a grown-up will help by being a referee.

- Do the *Great Save!* true or false quiz:

   • **Jonty's dad gave the team new football shirts.   T or F**

   • **Imran was the best goalkeeper.   T or F**

- **Mrs Roberts chose six children to be in the five-a-side team.   T or F**

- **The Greats won the football tournament. T or F**

- Draw and colour a big picture of the football match. There should be five players in each team. (The illustrations at the end of the story may help you with drawing the players in action.)

- Make up some words for a song to encourage a football team. The Red Fox is a singer. He suggests that the children record a song based on his words 'C'mon, you Greats! C'mon, you Greats!' Keep your song cheerful, try to use rhyming words at the end of the lines and repeat some phrases.

ALSO AVAILABLE AS COLOUR FIRST READERS

For My Great Mum!

GREAT SAVE!
A CORGI BOOK 978 0 552 56890 6

Published in Great Britain by Corgi Books,
an imprint of Random House Children's Publishers UK
A Random House Group Company

Corgi Pups edition published 1998
This Colour First Reader edition published 2013

1 3 5 7 9 10 8 6 4 2

The Random House Group Limited supports the Forest Stewardship Council (FSC®),
the leading international forest certification organization. Our books carrying the FSC
label are printed on FSC®-certified paper. FSC is the only forest certification scheme
endorsed by the leading environmental organizations, including Greenpeace. Our paper
procurement policy can be found at www.randomhouse.co.uk/environment.

MIX
Paper from
responsible sources
FSC® C013123

Set in Bembo MT Schoolbook 21pt/28pt

Corgi Books are published by Random House Children's Publishers UK,
61–63 Uxbridge Road, London W5 5SA

www.**randomhousechildrens**.co.uk
www.**totallyrandombooks**.co.uk
www.**randomhouse**.co.uk

Addresses for companies within The Random House Group Limited can be found at:
www.randomhouse.co.uk/offices.htm

THE RANDOM HOUSE GROUP Limited Reg. No. 954009

A CIP catalogue record for this book is available from the British Library.

Printed in Italy.

GREAT SAVE!

Rob Childs

Illustrated by Michael Reid